The KnowHow Book of Spycraft

Falcon Travis and Judy Hindley

Illustrated by Colin King
Designed by John Jamieson

Contents

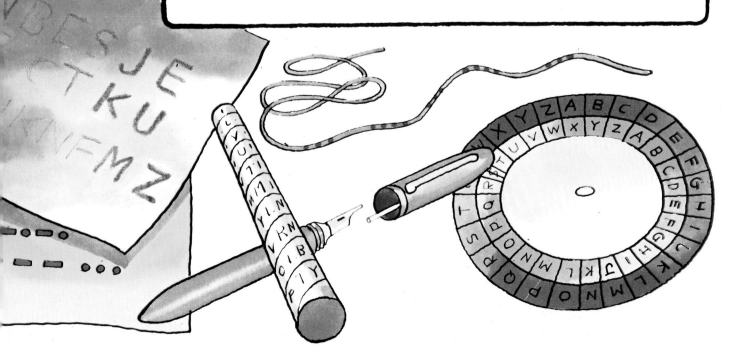

Carrying Secret Messages

One of the first spy tricks you should learn is how to deliver a secret message. Don't attract your enemy's attention by carrying a satchel or holding suspicious-looking papers. With the Stick Scrambler shown below you can encode a message on a paper strip that is easy to hide. See the chart for the methods used by Black Hat Spy for hiding messages.

Practise removing the message with a quick and casual-looking movement – as though you are just hooking your thumb in your pocket or taking a pebble from your shoe. If you hide the message in a pen or hat you can pretend to leave it somewhere by accident, and then your spy-friend can pick it up.

On the following pages you will find more details on where to hide your messages and how to pass them secretly to other spies.

Spy Language – A spy-friend is called a contact. A spy who carries messages is a courier. A spy who holds messages to be picked up is a 'letter-box'.

HIDING PLACES FOR MESSAGE

INSIDE HAT BAND

BETWEEN STRAPS

PINNED BEHIND LAPEL

INSIDE PEN

INSIDE CUFF

SECRET POCKET BEHIND FLAP

UNDER PLASTER REMEMBER-STICK THE PLASTER ON A PART OF THE BODY LIKELY TO GET SCRATCHED LIKE A HAND OR KNEE

INSIDE SOCK

UNDER FALSE SOLE OF SHOE

BLACK HAT SPY

1. Stick Scrambler

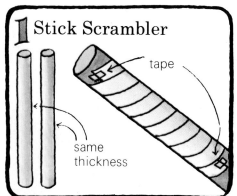

tape

same thickness

Both you and your contact must have sticks of just the same thickness. (Try pencils.) Wind a strip of paper tightly round your stick. Fasten it with sticky tape.

2

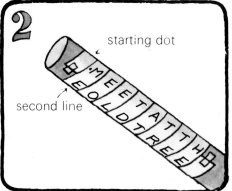

starting dot

second line

Write a message on the strip, like this. Make a dot beside the first letter to show your contact where the message starts. Turn the stick to add more lines.

3

Unwind the paper and the letters will be scrambled up. The message will be hidden until your contact winds the strip round a stick of exactly the same thickness.

False Sole

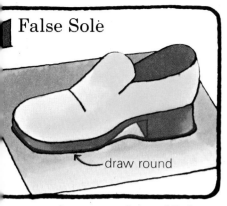

draw round

ut your shoe on a piece of light **rd**board, such as a piece of cereal **ck**age and draw around it.

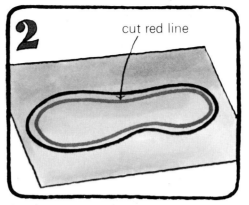

cut red line

Cut just inside this line to make a false sole that will fit inside your shoe.

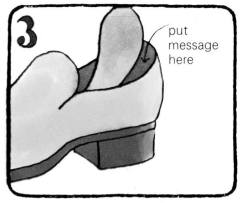

put message here

Slip the message between the real sole and the false sole as shown. Use this method if you think you might be stopped and searched by enemies.

Secret Pocket

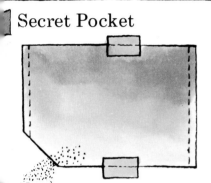

t off a corner of a tea-bag and **pty** out the tea. Make tabs of **cky** tape.

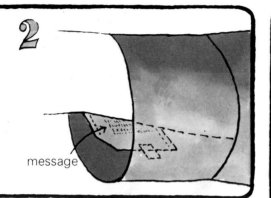

message

Stick the tea-bag in a hidden place, like the inside of a cap or sleeve. Fold the message very small and tuck it inside.

Spy Trick

THE SPY IS SEEN STANDING BESIDE THIS WALL. HE SEEMS TO BE INNOCENTLY READING A NEWSPAPER BUT IS HE?

Pen Message

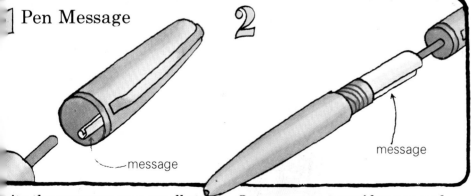

message

message

rite the message on a small strip **paper**. Roll the strip very tightly **d** keep it in the top of a pen.

Or unscrew a cartridge pen and wind the message strip around the ink cartridge. Then screw the pen together again.

SECRETLY, HE IS HIDING A ROLLED PAPER MESSAGE IN A CRACK IN THE WALL. LATER HIS CONTACT WILL PICK IT UP. TURN THE PAGE TO FIND MORE SPY TRICKS. ▶▶

Spy Post Office

A park is a good place to set up a secret post office. Spies often meet or leave messages in parks because you can wander or dawdle in a park without looking too suspicious. Most parks have open places where you can have a good look round to see if you're being followed. And your meetings with other spies can look very innocent and accidental. Follow the spy in the picture here to see some of the ways a spy post office works.

You can hide messages in all kinds of places if you make sure your contact knows where to look. But if you bury the message, put it in a small tin, like an elastoplast tin, or in a bottle, so that it won't get rain-soaked or chewed up by a nosey animal.

Spy Language – A place where you leave messages is called a 'drop'.

When on spy business, a good spy tries not to be seen twice in the same spot. Can you work out how a spy could get to all the message spots in the picture without re-tracing his steps? Clue – the letters on the picture spell the name of a car. Join them up correctly to find the trail.

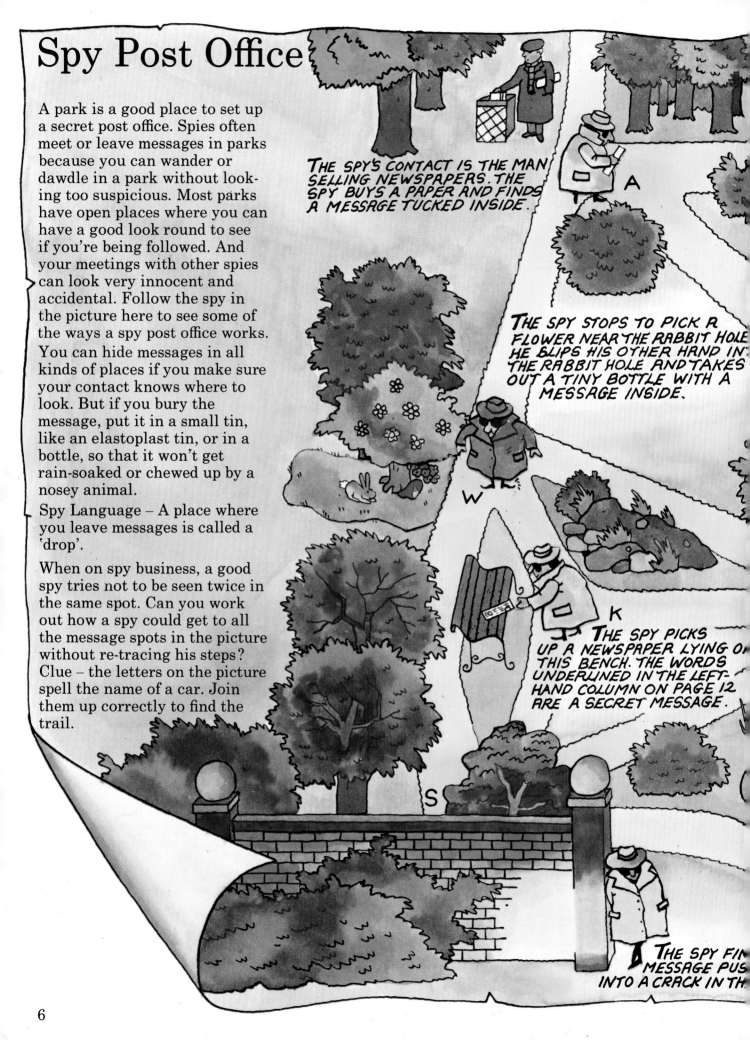

THE SPY'S CONTACT IS THE MAN SELLING NEWSPAPERS. THE SPY BUYS A PAPER AND FINDS A MESSAGE TUCKED INSIDE.

THE SPY STOPS TO PICK A FLOWER NEAR THE RABBIT HOLE. HE SLIPS HIS OTHER HAND IN THE RABBIT HOLE AND TAKES OUT A TINY BOTTLE WITH A MESSAGE INSIDE.

THE SPY PICKS UP A NEWSPAPER LYING ON THIS BENCH. THE WORDS UNDERLINED IN THE LEFT-HAND COLUMN ON PAGE 12 ARE A SECRET MESSAGE.

THE SPY FIN[DS A] MESSAGE PUS[HED] INTO A CRACK IN TH[E]

Whispering Wood

THE SPY STOPS AND PRETENDS TO SMELL THE FLOWERS. HE FINDS THE MESSAGE IN A SMALL BOTTLE PUSHED INTO THE SOIL.

THE SPY PICKS UP THIS UMBRELLA AND TAKES IT HOME. WHEN HE IS ALONE HE UNSCREWS THE HANDLE AND FINDS A MESSAGE INSIDE.

THE SPY KNEELS BY THIS TREE AND PRETENDS TO TIE HIS SHOE LACE. HE FINDS THE MESSAGE UNDERNEATH A TREE ROOT.

E SPY SITS DOWN ON THIS NCH AND FINDS A SSAGE STUCK UNDER THE NCH WITH A DRAWING PIN.

THE SPY PRETENDS TO STUMBLE AGAINST THIS LOG. HE STOOPS TO RUB HIS SHIN AND PULLS OUT A MESSAGE FROM BENEATH THE LOG.

HERE THE SPY MEETS A MAN WALKING A DOG. THE SPY SCRATCHES THE DOG'S HEAD AND FINDS A MESSAGE UNDER THE DOG'S COLLAR.

Quick Codes

You can make some very quick and easy codes just by making a few small changes in your messages. The best example is the Word-Split Code. Just split the words in a different way to make the message look completely different. For instance, the message 'We trail spies' can be changed to 'Wet rails pies.' In the code message all the letters are the same – only the spacing between the letters has been changed.

You can make other good codes by changing round the message letters in simple ways or adding dummy letters to the message. On the right you will find examples of these codes and clues on how to break each kind of code.

Find the Master Spy

The people you see in the picture below are QZ spies. Each has a message for you in one of the six codes shown on the right. Begin with the message at Start – each decoded message will lead you to another contact. Break all the codes to find which of your contacts was actually the Master Spy of the QZ Spy Ring.

Breaking the Codes

Try these methods on each message to work out which code was used.

1   Try joining the first code word to one or two letters of the second code word.

2   Spell the first few code words backwards.

3   Take away the first letter of each code word and see if the remaining letters make words.

4   Take away the last letter of each code word and see if the remaining letters make words.

5   Exchange the last letter of each code word with the first letter of the next code word.

1 Word-Split

WE|T RAIL|S PIES

First word Second word Third word

To break the code, join the letters a different way.

2 Backwards Words

EW LIART SEIPS

Spell each word backwards

To break the code, spell each code word backwards.

3 Backwards Sentences

SEIPS LIART EW

Spell sentence backwards

To break the code, spell the sentence backwards.

4 Dummy First Letter

QWET BRAI XLSP XIES

Take away first letter

To break the code, cross out the first letter of each 4-letter code word. Join up the remaining letters into words.

5 Dummy Last Letter

WETX RAIX LSPX IESX

Take away last letter

To break the code, cross out the last letter of each 4-letter code work. Join up the remaining letters into words.

6 Exchanged Letters

WETA RILP SIES

Exchange first and last letters

To break the code, exchange the last letter of each 4-letter code word with the first letter of the next.

Mystery Codes

The mysterious papers Black Hat is examining are coded messages. These pages show the key to each of them. Can you decode them?

Music Code

The key to the music code is at the right. It shows which note stands for each letter of the alphabet and for each of the numbers from one to nine. Use O for nought.

Match Black Hat's message notes with those in the key to find the letter that each note stands for. (The first letter of the message is W).

A dot marks the end of a word.

Pig-Pen Code

This mysterious-looking code is very easy to use. To make the key first draw the patterns shown here.

1 Railfence Code

To encode a message, first write the letters in an up-and-down pattern, on two lines. Add a null (extra letter) if needed to make both lines the same length.

2

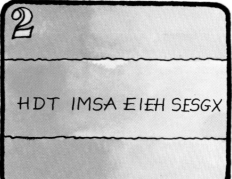

Now write out the letters of the first line, then the letters of the second line. Put them in groups, like words. Make sure your contact knows how to decode this.

3

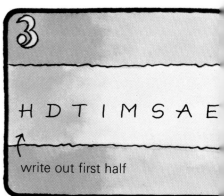

To decode a railfence message, first count out the first half of the message. Write it out with big spaces between the letters.

10

Key to Music Code

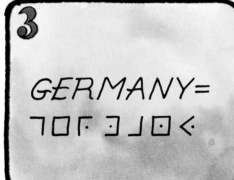

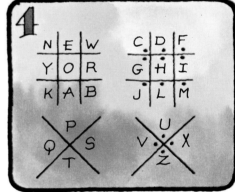

2
ow write in the letters of the
phabet like this. The pattern
lines or of lines and dots next
each letter is used to stand for
at letter.

3
This example shows how the
password 'Germany' looks in Pig-
Pen. Now see if you can work out
the secret message Black Hat has
found.

4
To make a more secret Pig-Pen
key, write the alphabet in a
different order. Start with a
keyword (a word with all-different
letters). Then add the rest of the
alphabet.

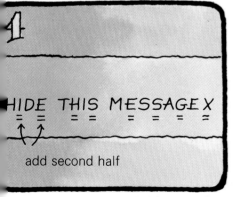

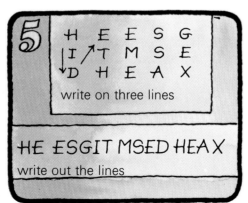

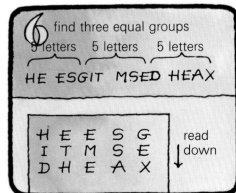

4
ow put the letters of the second
lf one by one into the spaces,
ke this. Try this method on the
cret message that Black Hat is
oking at.

5
To change the code, write the
letters in an up-and-down pattern
on three lines, like this. Then
write out the letters from each
line, as before.

6
To decode the message your
contact must count out three
equal groups of letters and write
them in three lines again. Then he
can read down each group of three.

Code Machines

With these machines you can encode and decode messages very quickly. The code strip shown below is easy to make. Use it to match the plain alphabet with a code alphabet that starts and finishes at a different letter. For example, start the code alphabet at B. Then change each plain letter for the one that follows it in the alphabet. Change the Z's to A's.

To make a code wheel, trace the pattern on page 13. Trace it carefully so that the alphabets line up when you spin the dial.

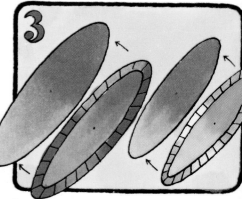

PTMVA HNM YHK LMKT
GZXK PBMA UETV DATM

This message is written in Code T. Match A with T on a code machine to break the code.

When you send messages, be sure your contact knows which code alphabet you have used.

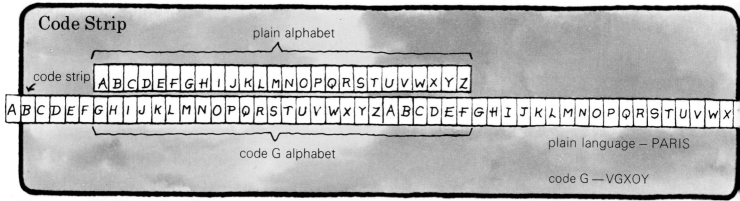

Code Strip

plain alphabet

code strip ← | A | B | C | D | E | F | G | H | I | J | K | L | M | N | O | P | Q | R | S | T | U | V | W | X | Y | Z |

| A | B | C | D | E | F | G | H | I | J | K | L | M | N | O | P | Q | R | S | T | U | V | W | X | Y | Z | A | B | C | D | E | F | G | H | I | J | K | L | M | N | O | P | Q | R | S | T | U | V | W | X |

code G alphabet

plain language — PARIS

code G — VGXOY

Mark a strip of paper into 26 spaces, one cm wide. Write the alphabet neatly in the spaces. Then mark 52 spaces, one cm wide, on a strip twice as long.

Write the alphabet twice in the spaces of the long strip, as shown above. Slide the short strip over the long strip to match the plain alphabet with a code alphabet.

For example, slide the short strip so that A stands over G to make Code G. Then match each plain letter with the letter beneath it on the code strip.

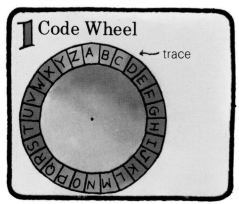

1 Code Wheel ← trace

Trace the red wheel from the pattern at the right. Trace the lines very carefully and mark the centre dot.

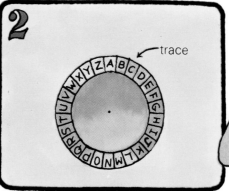

2 ← trace

Trace the blue wheel in the same way. Print one letter of the alphabet in each border space, on both wheels. Cut out the wheels.

3

Draw and cut out a wheel from light card (like a cereal package) and glue each paper wheel to a card wheel.

Top Secret

This is how to use two code alphabets. First print the message. Then print the names of the alphabets over and over to mark each plain letter. Set the code strip or wheel at P and encode all the letters marked P. Set it at Q to encode the rest. Tell your contact to decode with PQ.

	PQP	QPQPQ	PQP	QPQPQ	PQP
message	WHO	WEARS	THE	BLACK	HAT
code P	L D	T G	I T	A R	W I
code Q	X	M Q I	X	R Q A	Q
code PQ	LXD	MTQGI	IXT	RAQRA	WQI

Code Wheel Pattern

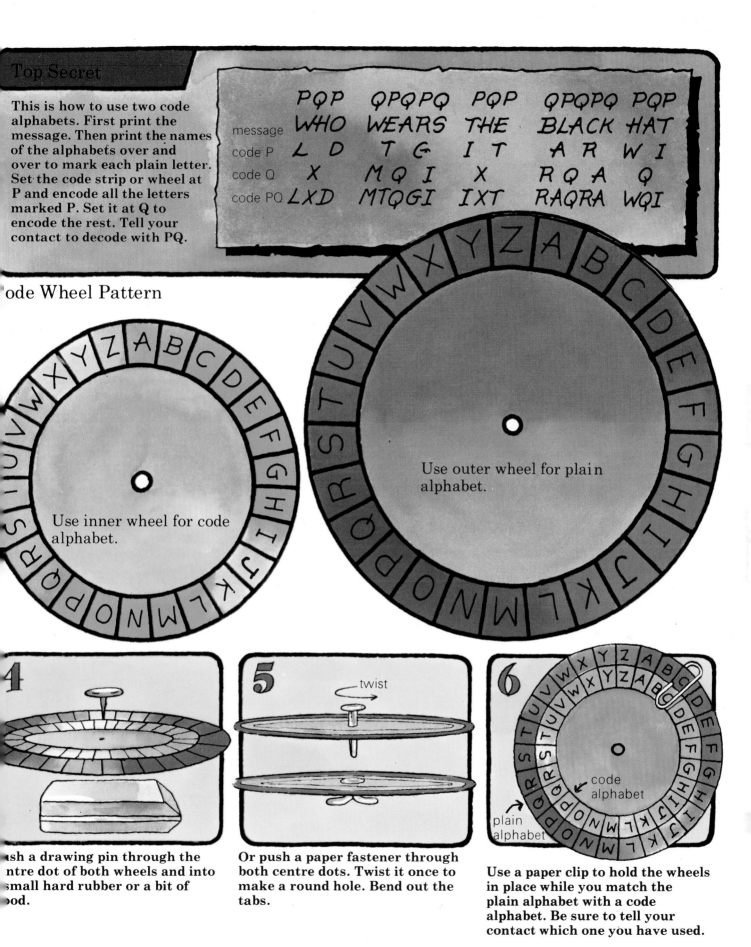

Use inner wheel for code alphabet.

Use outer wheel for plain alphabet.

4 ush a drawing pin through the ntre dot of both wheels and into mall hard rubber or a bit of ood.

5 twist — Or push a paper fastener through both centre dots. Twist it once to make a round hole. Bend out the tabs.

6 code alphabet — plain alphabet — Use a paper clip to hold the wheels in place while you match the plain alphabet with a code alphabet. Be sure to tell your contact which one you have used.

More Code Machines

S O L L T W
I T G I M S
L E O A P H
N O T S I W
N N S T A
E X L D A Y

Use a code grille to reveal the hidden message.

I Make the Grille

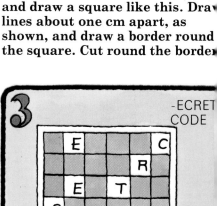

1 cm

1 cm {

six rows
across
and six
rows down

draw
border

Use light card, like a cereal box, and draw a square like this. Draw lines about one cm apart, as shown, and draw a border round the square. Cut round the border.

1 Encoding a Message

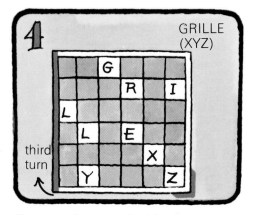

THIS
IS
HOW

mark
corner

Place the grille on some paper. Draw round one corner of the grille to mark its place. Print one letter of the message in each space as shown.

2

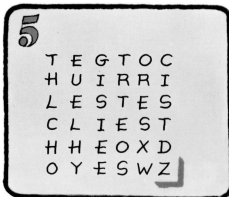

first turn

TO
USE
THE
S-

Now give the grille one turn clockwise so that the top edge becomes the right side. Match a corner with the corner mark. Fill the spaces with letters.

3

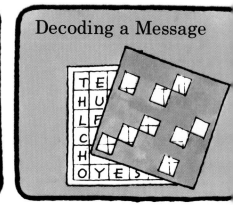

-ECRET
CODE

second turn

Give another clockwise turn so that the top edge becomes the bottom edge. Match the corner with the corner mark and fill the spaces with letters.

4

GRILLE
(XYZ)

G
R I
L
L E
X
Y Z

third turn

Turn again to make the top edge become the left side. Fill the rest of the spaces with letters. Add extra letters if needed to fill all the spaces.

5

T E G T O C
H U I R R I
L E S T E S
C L I E S T
H H E O X D
O Y E S W Z

When you lift the grille the message will look like this. Write it in a line, like this: Tegtoc huirri lestes cliest hheoxd oyeswz.

Decoding a Message

T E
H U
L E
C L
H H
O Y E S

First print the message in squares that match the grille. Place the grille over the message with the coloured edge at the top. Turn it to show all the letters.

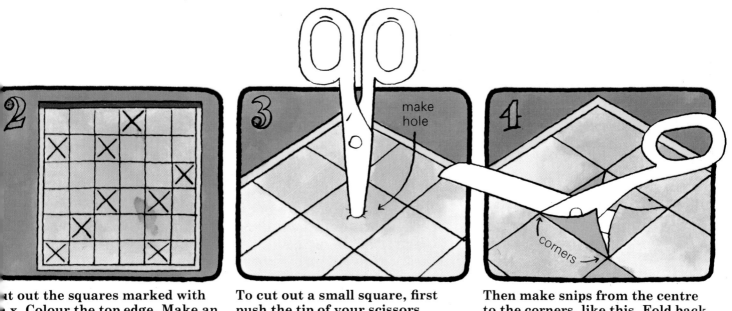

2 ...t out the squares marked with ...a x. Colour the top edge. Make an ...xact copy of the grille for your ...ntact.

3 To cut out a small square, first push the tip of your scissors through the centre of the square, as shown.

4 Then make snips from the centre to the corners, like this. Fold back the four triangles and cut them off.

1 Back-to-Front Grille

← top edge

front

...ere is a different pattern. ...old the grille as shown to ...gin. For the second step ...ve two clockwise turns so ...e top edge is at the bottom.

2

top edge

back

...r the third step turn the grille ...er. For the fourth step give two ...ockwise turns again, so that the ...p edge is at the bottom.

Super Code Grille

Trace this pattern to make a 144-letter code grille. With this code machine you can write a secret message almost as fast as an ordinary letter.

Black Hat Spy's Equipment . . .

Here is Black Hat in his attic den, surrounded by spy equipment. (You may recognize many of his tools – other pages in the book show how to make them.) Black Hat has just noticed that someone is climbing towards the attic on a ladder. It may be the window-cleaner – but it may be a spycatcher in disguise. In the next few minutes Black Hat must find a way to hide all the evidence that he is a spy. How can he do it?

On the right you can see how the spy den will look in just five minutes. Can you work out any of the tricks that Black Hat uses to hide his spy equipment? The answers are on the next page, upside-down.

AERIAL →

TUNER →

THE SPY DOES NOT KNOW HIS ROOM IS 'BUGGED'

PEN BARREL TWO LENSES

MICRODOT READER – THE TWO LENSES IN THE BARREL OF THE PEN CAN MAGNIFY THE DOT 200 TIMES

SHORT WAVE RADIO FOR SENDING SPY MESSAGES

MICRODOT-MAGNIFIED 200 TIMES TO SEE SECRET MESSAGE

CODE WHEEL (SEE PAGE 14)

HOLLOW RING WITH MINIATURE TAPE RECORDER

BOTTLE OF INVISIBLE IN

CODE BOOK-LIKE A FOREIGN DICTIONARY, WITH A SIGN OR NUMBER FOR EACH WORD OR MESSAGE THE SPIES MIGHT WANT TO SEND ALWAYS VERY TINY.

← SPY MAPS

nd How He Hides It Away

5 MINUTES LATER

Where is Black Hat's Spy equipment now? Turn the page upside-down to check your answers.

Bottle of invisible ink – inside teapot spout.

Microdot – on the side of the envelope that is turned down. A microdot has a special shine that a spycatcher might notice.

Microdot reader in pen barrel – put together as pen.

Code book – hidden in teapot inside small plastic bag with elastic band around it.

Hollow ring – on Black Hat's finger.

Radio – behind sliding panel disguised as book shelf. The books at the left end are real books. Those at the right are just pieces of book-cover stuck to the panel.

Code Wheel – hidden under lid of sugar bowl.

Binoculars – hidden under tea-cosy.

Maps – pushed into sleeves of coat, which are tucked into pockets to keep maps from sliding out.

Invisible Writing

A message in secret ink is usually written on the back of an ordinary letter or in the blank spaces between the lines and along the sides.

You will need

a piece of white candle and some fine powder for wax writing. You can use powdered instant coffee, chalk scrapings or even fine earth in an emergency

ink or paint and a brush or sponge to make the water message appear

a potato for the potato inkwell

some paper – use thin paper for the water mark

To make a pen that doesn't leave deep scratch marks, sharpen one end of a used match with a pencil sharpener, sandpaper or a nail file.

Remember – always mark the message to show your contact how to develop it (make it appear).

Marks to use are:

wx for a wax message

wm for a water message

h for a message that must be heated

× on the message side of the paper

sign for wax message

Know How
Spycatcher Club
Box (WX) 123

Dear Member,
To send a really secret message, use invisible writing and a code. Can you decode the password written between these lines? (Pig-Pen Code, page 138) Red chalk dust was used to make it appear. Notice the phone address – the letters W X are really a sign that the true message was written with wax.

1 Potato Inkwell

Hold the potato like this and cut off both ends with a table knife, as shown.

2

Stand the potato on one end. Scoop a hole in the top with a spoon.

3

scrape

Now use the blade of the table knife to scrape and squeeze the juice from the cut top of the potato into the hole.

4

Dip the sharpened end of a used match into the potato ink to write the message. When the 'ink' dries, the message will be invisible.

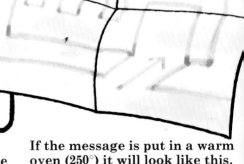

If the message is put in a warm oven (250°) it will look like this. Make other 'inks' with lemon jui milk, onion juice or coca-cola.

1 Water Writing

dry paper

write firmly

wet paper

Wet some paper thoroughly. Lay it on a smooth, hard surface. Cover with dry paper and write firmly. The message will appear on the wet paper when it is held to the light.

The message will vanish when the paper dries and reappear whenever it is wet. Your contact can brush it with watery ink or paint to make it permanent.

You can make water-mark messages on dry paper with a matchstick dipped in slightly soapy water. The soapy shine will help you see what you are doing.

1 Wax Writing

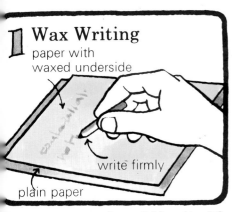

paper with waxed underside

write firmly

plain paper

Wax some paper by rubbing it with white candle. Then lay the waxed side on plain paper. Write firmly to print the message in wax marks on the plain paper.

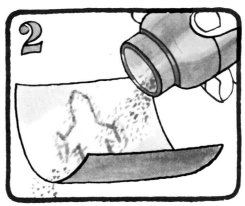

Your contact should sprinkle the message paper with powdered instant coffee or chalk scrapings or some fine dust.

When he gives the paper a gentle shake the powder will stick to the message and slide off the rest of the paper.

Spy Trick

BLACK HAT HAD JUST ARRIVED IN THE COUNTRY. AT THE AIRPORT HE WAS STOPPED AND SEARCHED, BUT WAS FOUND TO BE CARRYING ONLY...A SEWING KIT...

THE SPY WAS ALLOWED TO GO. AFTER ALL, A FEW NEEDLES AND COTTON CAN'T BE MUCH HELP TO THE ENEMY... OR CAN THEY?

ALONE IN HIS ROOM, THE SPY DREW THE COTTON OVER A HOT LIGHT BULB, AND TINY DOTS OF INVISIBLE INK APPEARED ALONG IT. TURN THE PAGE TO SEE HOW TO USE A DOT CODE.

19

Dot Code Messages

Dear Grandma
How are you? It is very nice in the country. Arthur got chased by a cow today. Albert got chased by a lot of bees. I am having a good time in the country. Love Frances
P.S. Here is Albert being chased by the bees.

| A | B | C | D | E | F | G | H | I | J | K | L | M | N | O | P | Q | R | S | T | U | V | W | X | Y | Z |

This letter is really a secret spy message. Each bee in the picture stands for one letter of the message. To find the message, first trace the code strip below the picture. Hold

the strip with its end right at the edge of the picture and slide it slowly down the page to match each bee with a letter. (The top bee stands for H.)

In this code each letter is made by dotting a piece of paper or a piece of string in a special place. A string message is easy to hide – you could even tie it round a parcel. And the dots on a piece of paper can be disguised inside a picture.

To encode a message you need a paper strip carefully printed with the alphabet. To decode the message your contact needs a strip just like yours. For extra secrecy use a keyword to scramble the letters of the alphabet.

Picture Dot Messages

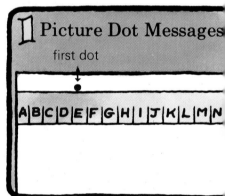

On this code strip you needn't leave space at start. Hold the strip near the top of a piece of paper. Put a dot over the first letter of the message.

Disguising the Dots

You can disguise the dot message as a picture. For example, you could turn the dots into birds, like this.

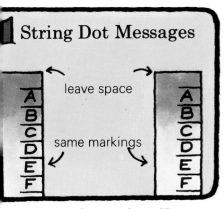

String Dot Messages

rk a strip of paper into 27
aces about one cm wide. Tell
ur contact to mark his strip the
me way. Leave a space and write
e alphabet as shown.

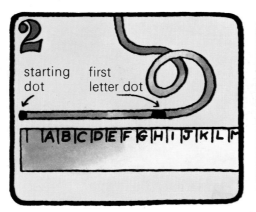

Make a starting dot at the end of a
piece of string. Hold the string
along the strip like this and dot it
with ink at the first letter of
the message.

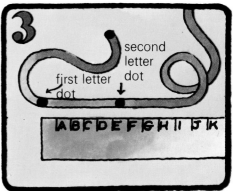

Move the first dot to the starting
point and make a second dot at the
second letter of the message. Move
each dot to Start before you make
the next dot.

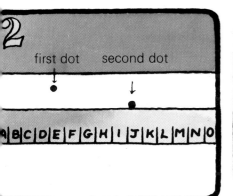

ove the strip down slightly and
t a second dot over the second
tter of the message. Continue
move the strip down to make
ch new dot.

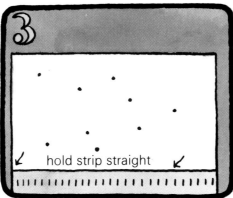

To decode the message your
contact moves his strip down the
page and 'reads' each dot. He must
hold the strip very straight, with
its end at the paper edge.

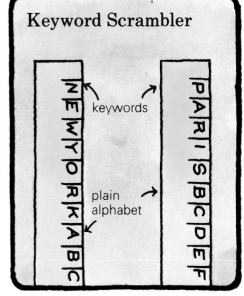

Keyword Scrambler

Suppose a lot of people know how
to use the ordinary code strip.
To keep them from reading your
messages make a special strip that
only you and your contact know
about. Choose a word with all-
different letters, like those above.
This will be your keyword. Write
the letters of this word in the first
spaces of the code strip. Then
write in the alphabet as before,
skipping the letters you have
already used.

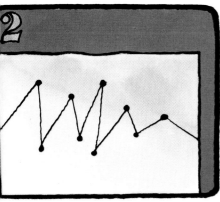

the dots could become points
a jagged line, to look like
rt of a chart.

You could even disguise the
message as a board game. The
snake's eyes here are the same
dots.

Quick Disguises

These quick disguises can help you fool your enemy. If your enemy is following you at a distance he will keep track of you by watching for something special about the way you look. Start out with a disguise that will catch his eye. Wear a bright scarf or a sling or use a special walk (see below). Then go into a shop or duck into a doorway and come out without it. Your enemy will be left wondering where you've gone.

Spy Language – Following is called 'shadowing' or 'tailing'. The person who does it is a 'tail' or 'shadow'.

Change Your Walk
A good spy trick is to pretend to have a stiff leg or a limp. But you might forget your stiff leg, or start limping on the wrong foot. Here are some ways to make sure you remember.
1   To make yourself limp, put a small stone in one shoe.
2   For a stiff leg, put a ruler at the back of one knee and tie it on with a scarf or string. Then you won't be able to bend it. Wear long trousers or a very long skirt to hide the ruler.

Arm in Sling

You will need a helper to put your arm in a sling. Use a big scarf or piece of cloth folded like this. Hold your arm across it and put a corner round your neck.

Lift the bottom corner and knot it to the piece round your neck. Then pin the side corner over your elbow, as shown.

One-Armed Spy

arm inside coat

sleeve in pocket

Wear your coat like this to look as though you only have one arm. Put one arm into a sleeve. Tuck the other sleeve into a pocket. Button the coat with one arm inside.

Two-Way Scarf

knot thread

take out pins after stitching

To make a quick-change scarf you will need two scarves the same size and shape but different colours. Pin them together like this and stitch around all four sides.

Change Your Shape

put on towel

with disguise

without disguise

hat and towel in bag

To raise your shoulders, lay a small towel behind your neck, like this. Then put a coat on over it. This will help you look like an older person with muscular shoulders.

To change your back view even more wear a hat or scarf as well. Take a folded carrier bag in your pocket. Later you can carry the hat and towel in the bag.

To make yourself look fatter, tie a small cushion round your middle. Button a coat on over it, or wear a very big jersey.

Change Your Looks

If your enemy knows you and is watching for you, try these tricks.

White Hair

Put talcum powder on your hair and eyebrows to whiten them. If you are fair they will go white and if you are dark they will go grey. Do just the front if you wear a hat.

Hair Combed Wrong Way

Comb your hair a different way. Slick it back or part it in a different place. If you have a fringe, comb it to the side.

Changed Eyebrows

Cover your eyebrows by rubbing bits of damp, soft soap into them. It might help to use face powder over the soap. Then draw new eyebrows with black crayon.

Face Colours

To make your face paler, rub some talcum powder on it. Rub it in gently and don't use too much. Use cocoa powder to make your face look browner.

Missing Tooth

From a distance, a blacked-out tooth looks like a gap. First wipe the tooth dry. Then rub black crayon over it.

5 O'clock Shadow

Mix daubs of blue and black paint with some face cream, like Pond's Cold Cream. Rub a little on your face like this, to look as though you need a shave.

Lumpy Face

Put small wads of cotton wool between your teeth and cheeks. Stick in lots to make fat cheeks. To make lumpy jowls just put them next to your lower teeth.

Wrinkle Lines

Draw wrinkle lines with a soft pencil, like a pencil marked 3B or 4B. Smile very hard, then wrinkle your forehead to see where the lines should go.

Spotting Clues

A spy must be very good at spotting clues. He has to get information from little signs and marks that other people would not notice. This page shows how to get information from footprints and from car and cycle tracks. This can be very useful if you lose sight of someone you are following. Sometimes the person you are following may disguise himself. Watch out for clues that can help you see through the disguise. Try the Spy Test below to see how good you are at spotting this kind of clue.

Tyre Track Clues

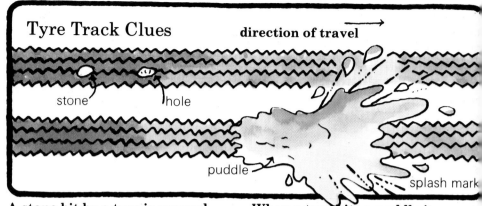

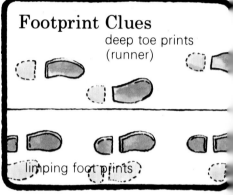

direction of travel

stone hole

puddle splash mark

A stone hit by a tyre is pressed down to make a hole and then kicked back. The marks left in the road show the direction in which the tyre was travelling.

When a tyre hits a puddle it splashes the oil or water forwards. Look for the splash-mark to work out which way the tyre was going.

Cycle Track Clues

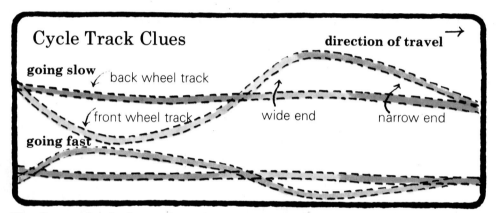

direction of travel

going slow back wheel track

front wheel track wide end narrow end

going fast

The front wheel of a cycle makes a loopy track, because the cyclist has to keep turning it to keep his balance. He turns less when going fast and makes smaller loops.

After turning the wheel, the cyclist straightens it, so the loops are always wider at one end than at the other. The narrow end points out where he is heading.

Footprint Clues

deep toe prints (runner)

limping footprints

If the person you are trailing is running, look for a deep toe print and light heel print. If he is limping, look for a deep footprint and then a light footprint.

Spy Test

SPY Z KNOWS A LOT OF DISGUISE TRICKS, BUT HE FORGETS TO HIDE ONE CLUE. READ ON AND SEE IF YOU CAN SPOT IT.

BLACK HAT HAS JUST SPOTTED SPY Z NEAR THE PALM HOTEL

AS SPY Z ENTERS THE HOTEL AND CALLS THE LIFT, BLACK HAT IS WATCHING. NOW IS HIS CHANCE TO SEE WHERE SPY Z HIDES OUT.

WHEN SPY Z ENTERS THE LIFT BLACK HAT RUNS UPSTEARS..

SLAM

Trapping Spies

Suppose you think that your enemy is getting into your secret hiding places. Set up one of the spy traps on this page and the intruder will be tricked into making a noise or leaving a clue that shows someone has been there. Door Trap No. 2 is particularly useful. Made with flour, it will leave a mark on anyone who who goes through the door.

You can make another good noise trap by sprinkling sugar on the floor. But people in socks or rubber soles can avoid this trap.

Hallway Trap

Tape a thin black thread from wall to wall, like this. Anyone who walks past this spot will make the thread fall down.

Desk Trap

clue mark

Spread some papers in a careless-looking way. Draw a tiny line that runs across two of them, like this. The smallest movement of the papers will break the line.

Door Trap No. 1

glued hair
(glue it low down or high up)

Glue a hair across the opening crack, like this. Check later – if someone has gone through the door, the hair will come unglued. Use the same trap on a drawer.

Door Trap No. 2

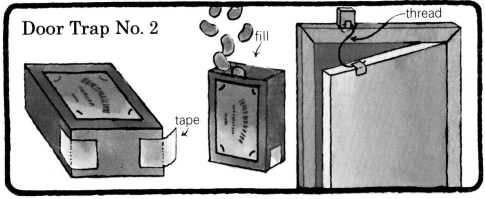

fill

tape

thread

Tape a bit of cardboard to one end of the cover of a matchbox to make a small, narrow box. Fill it with beans (for noise trap) or with flour (for marking trap).

Tape one end of a thread to the box. Then prop it on a door frame. Tape the thread to the door, like this, and close the door. If anyone opens it, the box will fall.

...AND REACHES THE FIRST FLOOR LANDING JUST IN TIME TO SEE A SECOND PERSON ENTER THE LIFT.

ON THE NEXT FLOOR, TWO MEN GET OUT. THIS IS THE TOP FLOOR — ONE OF THEM MUST BE SPY **Z** IN DISGUISE.

BLACK HAT FOLLOWS THE TWO MEN DOWN THE HALL. AS THEY TAKE OUT THEIR KEYS HE SEES THE CLUE THAT HE'S BEEN WAITING FOR. DO YOU? (SEE PAGE 31 TO FIND THE ANSWER)

Secret Telephone Messages

BLACK HAT PICKS UP THE TELEPHONE AND SAYS..

ZABI DAKIDO KUKADA BUKON OZO BUBIDU KOBA BI BAGU-BE

The code spoken by Black Hat is made by using the alphabet box on the next page. Each plain letter is replaced by two of the code letters in the frame. The code can be spoken because one of the two letters is always a vowel (a, e, i, o or u). Your contact should write down the code message as he hears it and decode it later.

Remember – be sure that you and your contact agree on how to say the vowels, or he may write down the wrong letter.

THE ENEMY, LISTENING, IS BEWILDERED.

① Encode your Message

H E L P

(double space below for writing code)

Print the plain message neatly. Leave space between each letter and between each line of letters.

②

H E L P
DO ZI NO GU

Replace each plain letter with the code letter on its row and the code letter on its column. Use strips of paper to line them up.

① Extra Security

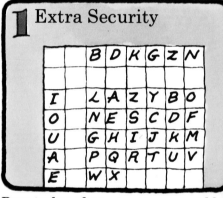

		B	D	K	G	Z	N
I		L	A	Z	Y	B	O
O		N	E	S	C	D	F
U		G	H	I	J	K	M
A		P	Q	R	T	U	V
E		W	X				

Remember that you can scramble the alphabet by starting with a keyword (a word with all-different letters). Then add the rest of the letters.

① Disguise Your Voice

To change your voice on the telephone, hold your mouth in a funny shape while you speak. For example, try to speak while holding a pencil in your teeth.

②

Now purse your lips as though you were going to whistle. Hold that shape while you speak. Try to speak in a normal voice and see what happens.

③

Now try a few more experiments. Try to speak while smiling very hard, as shown, or frowning.

1 Decode the Message

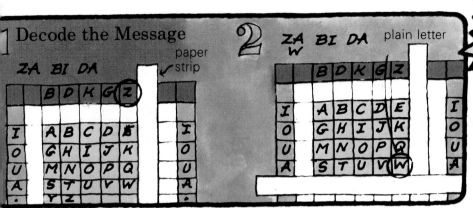

Write out Black Hat's message in pairs of letters. The first code letter is in one of the red squares that mark the columns. Mark the column with a paper strip.

You will find the second code letter in one of the blue squares that mark rows. Mark the row with a paper strip. The plain letter is where the two strips of paper meet.

use different code letters to mark the columns. You can use any letters except vowels (the letters that mark the rows).

try holding your nose while you practise the methods shown. You will find that your voice is completely different.

Alphabet Box

Make the code for each plain letter with one letter from a red square and one letter from a blue square.

The picture shows how to encode the letter K. It doesn't matter whether you say OZ or ZO.

Silent Signals

If you and your contact can see each other but cannot speak or get close enough to pass a message, signal with the Silent Alphabet shown on the page on the right. Or blink the Morse Code (see page 30) as shown below. In a crowded room or busy street you and your contact can send quick messages or warnings with Silent Hand and Leg Signals.

Silent Hand and Leg Signals

1   One hand in pocket – yes.
2   Two hands in pockets – no.
3   Scratching head – can you meet me at the hiding place?
4   Scratching back of neck – be careful. You are being watched.
5   Crossing legs – leave your message at the 'drop'.
6   Both hands behind back – I cannot pass the message now.
7   Scratching ear – I will telephone you later.
8   Standing on one leg – I'm going home now.

Morse Blink Signals

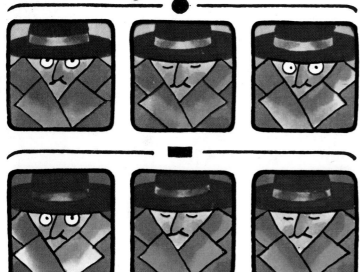

Blink for a count of one to make a dot and blink for a count of three to make a dash. A stare means the end of a word or message.

Morse Wink Signals

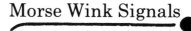

Wink to make a dot and blink to make a dash. A stare means the end of a word or message.

28

Silent Alphabet

On this page you can see how to make the letters of the alphabet with your hands. The pictures show how the hand signals should look to your contact. Don't practise in front of a mirror – the reflected signals will be the wrong way round. You and your contact should practise the signals together.

At the bottom of the page you will find some quick signs to make to answer questions or to tell your contact whether or not you understand his message.

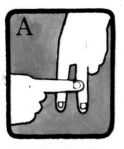 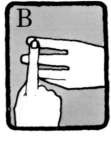  

 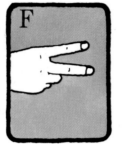 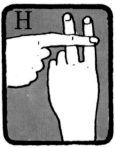

    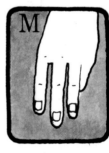 

     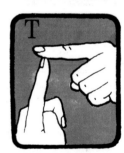

 Quick Signs

Yes

No

Understood

Not Understood

Repeat

29

Morse Code

Morse is a particularly useful code because it can be sent in so many different ways. You can signal it with a buzzer or a whistle or by flashing a torch on a dark night. Morse can also be tapped out or blinked with your eyes. This page shows the Morse code alphabet.

In this code a dot (·) stands for a short signal and a dash (−) stands for a long signal. To time the signals correctly, remember that a dash is always three times as long as a dot. For example, you should flash your torch for a count of one to make a dot and for a count of three to make a dash.

Don't run letters or words together. Between two letters wait for a count of three. Between two words, wait for a count of five.
Use the extra signals shown below to make sure that your contact is ready to receive your message and that he understands it.

Morse Alphabet

A · −	H · · · ·	O − − −	V · · · −
B − · · ·	I · ·	P · − − ·	W · − −
C − · − ·	J · − − −	Q − − · −	X − · · −
D − · ·	K − · −	R · − ·	Y − · − −
E ·	L · − · ·	S · · ·	Z − − · ·
F · · − ·	M − −	T −	full stop · − · − · −
G − − ·	N − ·	U · · −	question mark · · − − · ·

Sender's Signals

· − · −

This means 'I'm about to send a message'. Wait for the receiver to signal 'ready' before you start.

· · −

This means 'end of message'. If the receiver answers 'not understood', repeat the message.

· · · · · ·

This means 'mistake'. When you have mis-spelled a word, repeat the word.

Receiver's Signals

· −

This means 'ready to receive'. At the end of a message it means 'message understood'.

· · · · · ·

This means 'not ready to receive'. At the end of a message it means 'message not understood'.

Quick Signal Code

This is a special code to use for signalling if you don't have time to learn the whole Morse or semaphore alphabet. With this code you can send any message with just six signals.

The code is made with an alphabet box, like the one used for secret telephone messages (pages 26 - 27). Each plain letter is replaced by the two code letters that line up with it in the frame of the box. But this time there are just six different code letters in the frame. They are written in capitals at the side and in small letters at the top of the box. The code pair should start with a capital. For example, the code pair used for R is Oi.

Learn the Morse or semaphore signals for the six letters used. Encode the message before you start signalling. Your contact should write down the code message as he receives it and decode it later.

To make the code more secret, start the plain alphabet with a keyword, like 'crazy'. Then add the other letters of the alphabet.

Telephone Messages
You can read off the code pairs like this. Say 'adle' for A, 'edle' for E, 'idle' for I, 'odle' for O, 'yewdle' for U, and 'ydle' for Y.

If you turn the coded message into Morse you can read it out by saying 'iddy' for a dot and 'umpty' for a dash. Remember to wait for a count of three between two letters. Between two words, wait for a count of five.

Alphabet Box

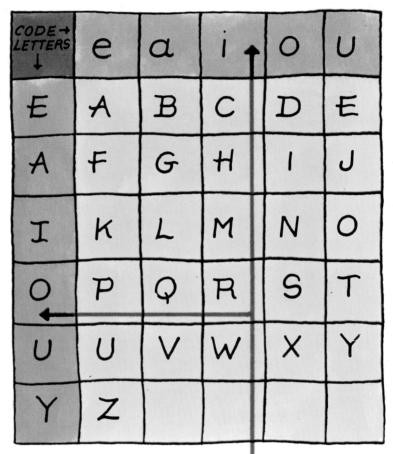

Replace each plain letter with the capital letter on its row and the small letter on its column.

Always start with a capital. For example, the code pair for R is Oi.

Break the Code

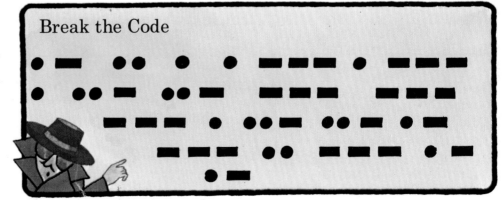

Here is a message Black Hat has just encoded, ready for signalling. Can you break the code?

Remember – the first letter of each code pair comes from the side of the box.

Spy Language

bug – a very small microphone hidden in a room so that people talking in that room can be overheard by the enemy.

contact – a spy friend, particularly one you meet by arrangement.

courier – a spy who carries secret messages or who carries orders from master spy to spy.

dead – 'Victor is dead' means 'Victor has been caught by the enemy'.

dead-letter box – hiding place for secret messages.

drop – hiding place for secret messages.

ill – 'Victor is ill' means 'Victor is being watched by the enemy'.

letter-box – a person who holds secret messages for spies to pick up.

master spy – head of a spy ring.

plain language – a message is in plain language when it has not been encoded.

shadow – someone who is following or 'shadowing' another person.

spy ring – a group of spies who work together. The master spy gives the orders, the couriers carry the orders to the spies, and the spies carry out the orders.

tail – someone who is following or 'tailing' another person.

Answers

Pages 2-3 — There are four secret passwords on these pages
They are 'Washington', 'Madrid', 'Paris' and 'Bologna'. Can you find them? (Use pig-pen and a code wheel.)

Pages 6-7 — The clue to the Spy Post Office Trail is 'Volkswagen'.

Pages 8-9 — Here is what the Quick Code Messages say:

At start – 'Meet girl in red hat at clock tower.'
At clock tower – 'Talk about roses to flower seller at fountain.'
At fountain – 'Ask man at statue for light for cigar.'
At statue – 'Stand near church door till old man arrives.'
At church – 'Wait under tree for lady with white cat.'
At tree – 'Man with arm in sling waits on bridge.'
At bridge – 'Buy a dictionary at the book stall and open at page 10.'
At book stall – 'Master Spy was the one you last met.'

Page 10 — The music code message says, 'We leave tonight.' The pig-pen code message says, 'Send new code immediately.' The railfence code says, 'Change the password.'

Page 12 — The message in Code T says, 'Watch out for stranger with black hat.'

Page 14 — The code grille message says, 'Light in east top window means all is lost.'

Page 18 — The password between the lines is 'Coca-Cola'.

Page 20 — The message made the bees is 'Help is on the way.'

Pages 24-25 — The first few pictures show that the spy is left-handed. The left-handed man in the last picture is the spy, wearing a disguise.

Pages 26-27 — Black Hat is saying, 'Watch out – milkman is a spy.' His contact answers, 'I knew it – the milk is sour.'